D1529286

TAKE ME TO
YOUR WEEDER

For my truly terrific tellurian family pod:
Ann, Ramsey, & Wink
—K.M.

Dedicated to all fellow lovers of plants, the most
interesting alien life forms I've ever encountered
—J.W.

Text copyright © 2016 by Kimberly Morris
Illustrations copyright © 2016 by Jessica Warrick
Galaxy Scout Activities illustrations copyright © 2016 by Kane Press, Inc.
Galaxy Scout Activities illustrations by Nadia DiMattia

Library of Congress Cataloging-in-Publication Data

Morris, Kimberly.
Take me to your weeder / by Kimberly Morris ; illustrated by Jessica Warrick.
     pages   cm. — (How to be an earthling ; 3)
     Summary: "Jack doesn't want the responsibility of watching the
class pet over the weekend so he leaves the hamster with Spork, the
new alien at school"— Provided by publisher.
ISBN 978-1-57565-825-4 (pbk) — ISBN 978-1-57565-824-7 (reinforced library
binding) — ISBN 978-1-57565-826-1 (ebook)
[1. Extraterrestrial beings—Fiction. 2. Responsibility—Fiction. 3. Schools—Fiction.
4. Humorous stories.] I. Warrick, Jessica, illustrator. II. Title.
PZ7.M7881635Tak 2016
[Fic]—dc23
2015023480

3 5 7 9 10 8 6 4 2

First published in the United States of America in 2016 by Kane Press, Inc.
Printed in China

Book Design: Edward Miller

How to Be an Earthling is a trademark of Kane Press, Inc.

Visit us online at **www.kanepress.com**

Like us on Facebook
facebook.com/kanepress

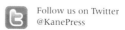
Follow us on Twitter
@KanePress

CONTENTS

***Don't miss a single one
of Spork's adventures!***

TAKE ME TO YOUR WEEDER

by Kimberly Morris
illustrated by Jessica Warrick

KANE PRESS
New York

Spork

Trixie Lopez

Mrs. Buckle

Jack Donnelly

Grace Hanford

Jo Jo

Newton Miller

REPORT TO TROOP

BEEP!
Ack! Ack! Cough! . . .
Spork here. Broadcasting from . . .
Ack! Ack! Cough! . . . Earth.
Sorry, guys! I'm eating something. Man, is it dry!

You know, I'm learning so much about Earth food, I'm practically an expert. Today my class is going to weed our garden and harvest some beans. Beans are these long green things that look like they should wiggle. But they don't.

It's amazing how many weird looking things on this planet turn out to be food.

Okay! Gotta go. My teacher, Mrs. Buckle, says breakfast is the most important meal of the day. So I want to finish this gravel before the bell rings.

Over and . . . Ack! Ack! Ack!
Cough!
BEEP!

1

FOOD, GLORIOUS FOOD

"How long before lunch?" Jack grumbled. He smushed a mud clod with his toe. Smushing mud clods was the only thing Jack liked about working in the school garden.

"*Ack! Ack! Ack! Cough.*" That was Spork, the new alien in class. All of a sudden Jack heard a horrible choking sound.

He looked at Spork. *Something was stuck in his throat!*

Mrs. Buckle ran to help, but Newton was faster. He wrapped his arms around Spork's rib cage and squeezed.

A pinecone shot out of Spork's mouth and hit the fence. *BAM!*

After that came a spray of gravel. *Rat tat tat tat tat.*

"Wow, Newton! That was awesome!" said Trixie.

"You're a hero!" said Mrs. Buckle.

All the other kids cheered.

Mrs. Buckle made sure Spork was okay. Then she asked, "Why are you eating pinecones and gravel? They're not food."

Spork looked puzzled. "Yesterday you said *everything* is food. Remember? When we talked about the food chain? Worms are food. Fish are food. Plants are food. Even wood is food."

"But not everything is food for *people,*" said Mrs. Buckle kindly.

"Worms are food for birds," Trixie said, yanking on a weed. "Fish is food for people."

"Unless it's a goldfish," Grace added. "Then it's a pet. You don't eat a pet."

Spork looked even more puzzled.

"Wood is food for termites," Newton explained. "And some plants are food for people. But lots of plants aren't and can make a person sick."

"But I am a not a human person,"

Spork answered. "I'm a space person, and I'm trying to learn what foods are right for me." He picked up a muddy stick and licked it. "Mmm. Not bad."

Jack laughed. "Ha, ha! Spork is eating mud."

"Don't laugh," Grace said. "I bet you ate some weird things before you learned about food."

"Did not," Jack argued.

"You ate a pill bug in Pre-K," Newton said. "I remember."

"Everybody likes different foods," said Mrs. Buckle. She took a bite of raw bean and made a loud silly crunching noise. "But nothing tastes better than fresh food you pick yourself."

"I still don't see why we have to pick

all these beans," Jack grumbled.

"Because the beans are the third grade's responsibility," Mrs. Buckle said. "Who can explain what *responsibility* means?"

Jack tried to come up with a good definition. But Trixie answered before he could think of anything. "Doing what you said you would," she said.

"That's right," said Mrs. Buckle. "And we said the third grade would pick beans to serve for lunch on Monday."

Jack began to feel very cranky. Trixie had answered Mrs. Buckle's question about responsibility before he could. And Newton, the big hero of the day, had told everybody he ate a pill bug.

Mrs. Buckle smiled at Jack. "Here's something that will make you happy, Jack. It's your turn to take Jo Jo home."

Jo Jo was the class pet. The students took turns keeping her on weekends.

"Hamsters are boring," Jack said. He actually liked Jo Jo a whole lot. But he was cranky, and it felt good to say mean things. "Why can't we have an interesting class pet? Like an elephant. Or a monkey. Or a moose?"

"I've seen pictures of elephants and monkeys," Spork said. "But what's a moose?"

"A humongous animal that lives in the woods. I saw one once when we were camping up north of here," said Grace. "It was scary!"

"Even a little baby moose would be more interesting than a hamster." Jack stomped hard on a mud clod to show his disgust.

Mrs. Buckle laughed. "I suppose that's true Jack. But we don't have a moose. So Grace, would *you* like to take Jo Jo home?"

"Yes!" Grace said. "I like to count how many seeds she stores in her cheeks. Last time I counted twenty-seven."

"Not fair!" Jack protested. "It's my turn!"

"But you said you didn't want to," Grace pointed out.

"Did not," Jack argued. "I just said hamsters are boring. It's still my turn."

"All right, Jack," said Mrs. Buckle. "You can take Jo Jo home."

Now Jack was mad at Grace for trying to take his turn. "Grace is a teacher's pet," Jack whispered to Spork, even though he knew that wasn't true.

"Teacher's pet?" Spork repeated thoughtfully. "What is a teacher's pet?"

Jack got a funny feeling in his tummy—the way you do when you think maybe you said something wrong. But then the bell rang. And by lunchtime, he had forgotten all about it.

2

GONE CAMPING

"Thirty-two. Thirty-three." That afternoon, Jack was in his bedroom watching Jo Jo take seeds out of her dish and put them in her mouth.

"Thirty-four. Thirty-five." Jo Jo's cheek pouches got bigger and bigger.

Wow! Jo Jo was breaking her own record.

Jack's mother came in. "Uncle Raul just called. He's taking the boys camping this weekend. He wants to know if you would like to go."

Jack jumped to his feet. "YES!"

The "boys" were Jack's twin cousins Hector and Sam. They were one year older and totally fun. Jack pulled his duffel bag out of the closet and started to pack. Swimsuit. Flip-flops. Underwear. Rubber snake. Whoopee cushion.

Wait a minute. What about Jo Jo? He couldn't go camping if he had to take care of Jo Jo. But who could he get to watch her?

He didn't want to ask Grace. Or Newton. Or Trixie. Not after he had made such a fuss about how it was his turn.

Suddenly Jack had a great idea. He knew exactly who could keep Jo Jo for him.

He put Jo Jo's tank in his wagon and pulled it to Spork's spaceship. He knocked, and the top flipped open.

Spork stuck out his head. His cheeks looked weird, all big and bulgy. "Wexhmmphhhlleee. Mssph. Hsempohlel. Phhlmm," Spork said.

"Why is your face swollen?" Jack asked.

Spork spit a HUGE pile of peas into his hands. "I'm experimenting with food storage," he said when his face was back to normal. "Jo Jo stores food in her cheeks. I thought that might work for me, too."

Normally Jack would have enjoyed teasing Spork. But today he didn't have time.

"I was thinking," Jack said quickly. "It's not fair for me to have Jo Jo again for the weekend. You've never had

even one turn. So I brought her over. It'll be fun, and you'll learn about responsibility."

"Cosmic!" said Spork. "Tell me what to do."

Jack handed Jo Jo's cage to Spork. "It's real easy. Just clean her tank and make sure she has fresh food. Some of these seeds. And stuff from the garden.

I'll be back to pick her up on Monday before school."

"Okay! Thanks for helping me," Spork said happily.

"Don't mention it," said Jack. Then he turned and ran away before Spork could ask him a bunch of questions.

Explaining stuff was hard work. No wonder Mrs. Buckle looked so tired by Friday!

3

BACK TO BEANS

On Monday morning, Jack arrived at Spork's spaceship before school. He was in a great mood. The camping trip had been tons of fun.

They had swum in the river. They had cooked hotdogs over the fire. They had played Jack's favorite board game, and Jack won three times in a row.

Jack had hardly argued at all with Hector. And he only got pantsed twice. Once for bragging. Once for putting the rubber snake in Sam's sleeping bag.

After that, he had decided not to use the whoopee cushion. But he still had it inflated and ready in his backpack. He was going to put it on Spork's chair at lunch. Heh! Heh! Heh!

Jack knocked on Spork's spaceship. The top lifted, and Spork popped out. He held up Jo Jo's tank. "Here you go. Clean as clean can be. I treated it with protonized Klozidion beams."

"But where's Jo Jo?" Jack asked.

Spork shrugged. "I don't know. I let her out so she could pick her own food. Fresh."

"When?" Jack asked.

"On Friday, after you left."

Jack felt a giant *WHOMP* in his stomach. "That was *three days ago*!"

"Time sure flies!" said Spork, climbing out of the spaceship.

"But . . . but . . . you were supposed to keep her in her tank."

Spork blinked in surprise. "I was? You didn't say that."

Ding, ding, ding went the school bell.

Spork smiled. "I'm glad it's Monday. I can't wait to eat some of those fresh beans at lunch."

Jack's good mood was gone. His heart was pounding, and his feet were as heavy as lead. He liked Jo Jo. He didn't want anything bad to happen to her.

He didn't want anything bad to happen to *him* either. And this was the kind of thing that could get him in big trouble.

Spork put the empty tank in Jack's

arms and gave him a nudge. "Come on." Jack stumbled along, trying to think. What should he say? What should he do?

Mrs. Buckle greeted them inside the classroom. "Good morning, Spork. Good morning, Jack." She smiled. "How is Jo Jo?"

Jack's mouth was dry. "Well, it's like this. Everybody likes taking Jo Jo home. And everybody's had at least one turn. Except for Spork. So I, uhhh, thought how Spork is trying to learn about Earth customs. And responsibility. And beans. And, uh . . ." Jack's mind went blank. What was his point?

"Where is she?" Trixie asked, peering at the empty tank.

"Jack let me keep Jo Jo," Spork said. "But I didn't know she was supposed to stay in her tank. So I let her go outside."

"*Outside* outside?" Newton croaked. "Where there's cats? And hawks? And owls? Oh, no! She's completely helpless. They might eat her!"

"Eat her?" Spork repeated. Then he slapped his orange forehead. "*Now I see my mistake. Jo Jo is food*! I was supposed to eat Jo Jo."

"NO!" everybody in the class shouted at once.

"Jo Jo is the class pet," Mrs. Buckle explained. "We don't eat pets. We take care of them. They are our responsibility."

Spork frowned. "I'm confused. You said the beans were our responsibility. But we're eating them for lunch. Aren't we?"

Jack looked around the group. "You see? It's not my fault! It's Spork's fault. He doesn't understand stuff!"

Spork looked sad. "I'm sorry."

"It's not your fault, Spork," said Mrs. Buckle. "Jo Jo was Jack's responsibility."

"Oh. I see. *Jack* was supposed to eat Jo Jo?"

"NO!" everybody in the class shouted again.

"Jo Jo is a *pet*," Trixie repeated.

"Like Grace is
the teacher's pet,"
said Spork.

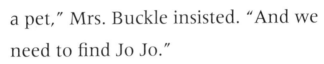

"NO!" the whole
class shouted again.

"I do *not* have
a pet," Mrs. Buckle insisted. "And we
need to find Jo Jo."

"Great!" Spork said in a happy voice.
"I've been wanting to work on my
Search and Rescue badge. But first I
have a surprise. Follow me!"

4

A NEW CLASS PET

Spork led the class to the cafeteria. "Jack said hamsters are boring. So I brought a pet that everybody said was interesting." Then he threw open the kitchen door and made a squeaky "ta da!" sound.

"Oh, dear," Mrs. Buckle said weakly.

Standing in the school kitchen was a baby moose calf.

"I looked up 'moose' on my podputer Friday night and found this guy over the weekend," Spork explained proudly.

The calf had chomped on just about everything in the kitchen. A big pot was covered with teeth marks. The refrigerator door was open. Broken eggs slithered across the floor on a sea of spilled milk.

"Oh, no!" Jack groaned.

"He's eating all the beans," said Grace.

"And the lettuce," said Newton.

"And the radishes," said Trixie. "And the juice boxes. And the mixing spoons."

The moose calf saw the children and began to moo.

"Don't worry," said Spork. "He's not humongous. He's just a baby. I don't know why he's still hungry, though. I made a trail of beans and lettuce and radishes all the way from the middle of the woods to right here."

The door opened, and in came a cafeteria worker. "HEY!" she shouted. "Get out of my kitchen."

The calf let out a terrified *BRAY!* and took off running.

Jack took off after it, his backpack thumping against his shoulders. Spork, Newton, Trixie, and Grace followed right behind.

The calf ran down the hall.

He ran past the fifth grade.

He ran past the fourth grade.

He ran past the third grade.

He turned left.

He turned right.

He ran into the boys' bathroom.

And then right back out again.

He ran into the girls' bathroom.

And then right back out again.

He ran to the end of the hall, charged

into the library, and galloped right through the kindergarten story circle.

"*WHOOAAAAA!*" Kindergarteners scattered in all directions.

CRASH!

The moose calf ran down the rows of bookshelves and knocked them over.

CRASH! went the picture books.

CRASH! went the chapter books.

CRASH! went the biographies.

CRASH! went the science books, the poetry books, the A to Z Illustrated Dictionary for kids, and all one hundred and twenty-five volumes of the HERE'S HOW how-to book series for readers six to nine.

BANG!

BOOM!

And . . . ***CRASH! BANG! BOOM!*** went the six-foot tall scale model of Mount Rushmore made out of cotton balls, packing peanuts, and potting clay.

"AHHGHGHGHGHGH!" screamed the kids as the calf turned to face them.

5

MOOSE ON
THE LOOSE

Everybody in the library jumped up on a table or hid underneath one.

Everybody except Jack. He was in the worst possible place at the worst possible moment. Face-to-face with the moose calf.

The calf flared his nostrils. He pawed the ground.

The library fell completely silent. No one wanted to make even the tiniest sound. Up close, the baby moose didn't look like such a baby. In fact, he looked pretty darned big. He gave Jack a very mean look.

"Don't move," Spork whispered. "I'll scare him off." He picked up a rubber

eraser and threw it at the calf. But he missed. The eraser bounced off the bookshelf and hit Jack in the middle of the forehead.

"Ow!" said Jack. He stumbled and fell backward, landing on his backpack.

FWAAAAAAAAAPP . . . PPP . . . PPP . . . PPP . . . PPP . . . PPP . . . PPP . . . PPP . . . PPP . . . PPP . . . PPP . . . PPP . . . PPP . . . PPP . . . PPP . . . PPP !!!!

The whoopee cushion in Jack's backpack sounded like a tuba blowing a raspberry.

The calf let out a terrified bray, leaped over Jack, and took off.

At the exact same moment, Trixie and Grace opened the double doors that led outside.

Before the last gassy, brassy note came to an end, the calf was halfway across the yard.

"Look, he's going toward the garden!" Trixie shouted.

Everybody ran outside.

The calf thundered through the neatly tended beds. Clouds of dirt, weeds, and vegetables swirled around his feet. Then

he ran out the school gate and into the woods.

"That's one way to weed the garden," said Newton.

Everybody laughed and breathed a sigh of relief.

Mrs. Buckle gathered them all up in a big hug.

But Jack stood aside.

He still had a major problem. Jo Jo. *Where would a hamster go?* he wondered. Hamsters weren't that adventurous. All Jo Jo did was sleep and eat and . . .

Jack snapped his fingers. *"Vegetables! That's it!"*

Jack raced across the schoolyard. He found what was left of Spork's vegetable trail. He trotted along it until he saw a big green lettuce leaf. It was *moving*!

"Is that a turtle?" asked Trixie, joining him.

"If it is, it's a lettuce turtle." Jack laughed. He lifted up the large lettuce leaf. There was Jo Jo! She was right underneath, munching on a bean.

Mrs. Buckle ran over and scooped up the hamster. The kids gathered around and took turns stroking her tiny head.

"Jo Jo may be boring," Grace said. "But she sure is sweet."

"Like ice cream?" Spork said brightly.

"NO!" said Jack, Newton, Trixie, Grace, and Mrs. Buckle.

One of the cafeteria workers stood in the open doorway. "I want to know who's going to clean up the kitchen? It's a disaster!"

"And who is going to pick up all the books?" asked the librarian.

"I will," Spork said.

"Can't we just use some Gloop?" asked Trixie.

Mrs. Buckle looked doubtful. "Better

not. Sometimes Gloop 'fixes' things we don't want 'fixed.' We've had enough surprises for one day."

"I'll help Spork clean up," Jack said quickly. Then he mumbled, "And I'm sorry." He was. Not just because he was in trouble. He felt bad about everything.

"First let's put Jo Jo in her tank," Mrs. Buckle said. "Then we'll ALL help Spork and Jack clean up."

After Jo Jo was settled in, Spork gave the group a sad smile. "You know, I've been thinking. Maybe I should try visiting a different Earthling Training Center. I keep making trouble for you."

Jack wished he could go to another "training center," too. *Actually, changing schools is a great idea,* he thought. *I'll talk to my parents tonight.*

"Please don't go, Spork. You're our friend. And everybody makes mistakes," Grace said. "Even Jack."

"Especially Jack," Trixie corrected.

Out of habit, Jack started to say, "DO NOT!" But he stopped himself. This time Trixie was right.

"Friends have a responsibility to help each other learn from mistakes,"

Mrs. Buckle said. "You can't learn anything if you run away."

Mrs. Buckle was looking at Spork, but Jack knew she was talking to him.

"Please don't go," everybody said again.

"Okay," Spork agreed happily.

Okay, Jack thought.

"Besides, you're both heroes!" Trixie told them.

"We are?" squeaked Spork.

"We are?" Jack echoed. "How? I mean, why?"

JACK   **SPORK**

"You scared away the moose," Newton said.

"You found Jo Jo," Grace added.

"And because of you guys," Trixie said with a grin, "we're probably the only people in the world who can say we were saved by a whoopee cushion!"

Jack smiled. Hero. It was a lot of responsibility. But he could get used to that.

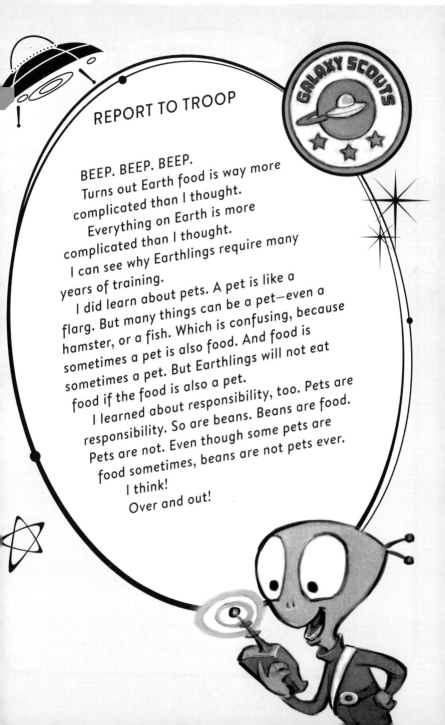

REPORT TO TROOP

BEEP. BEEP. BEEP.
Turns out Earth food is way more complicated than I thought. Everything on Earth is more complicated than I thought. I can see why Earthlings require many years of training.

I did learn about pets. A pet is like a flarg. But many things can be a pet—even a hamster, or a fish. Which is confusing, because sometimes a pet is also food. And food is sometimes a pet. But Earthlings will not eat food if the food is also a pet.

I learned about responsibility, too. Pets are responsibility. So are beans. Beans are food. Pets are not. Even though some pets are food sometimes, beans are not pets ever. I think!

Over and out!

Greetings!

Wait until you hear about responsibility! It's about doing things you said you'd do—and kind of thinking ahead so you don't do anything that makes trouble for somebody (or yourself!). Here's a quiz you can take to see if you get the idea. Good blatz!

—Spork

(There can be more than one right answer.)

1. You have a big test on Gloop Power tomorrow.
   a. You stay up all night studying.
   b. You stay up late playing Karx with your friends.
   c. You take out your Gloop Power textbook and study for two hours.
   d. You take out your Gloop Power textbook and decide to take a nap. (You wake up the next morning ten minutes before the test.)

2. You're ready to take off on your next assignment—to get a rush supply of the metal blix. You've been told it can only be found on the planet Thaxos. Or—wait a minute—was it Paxos?
   a. Go to both planets.
   b. Look it up in Guide to the Galaxy.
   c. Pretend you have space flu.
   d. Ask your Leader which planet is the right one.

3. You borrowed a kicklride from a friend and can't find it. (This really happened to me!) What would you do?
   a. If you see her, go the other way.
   b. Make up a story—like a space monster attacked you and ran off with it.
   c. Tell her you're really sorry.
   d. Tell her what happened and say you'll get her another one.

4. You lose your flarg.
   a. Yell, "Somebody stole my flarg!"
   b. Examine every flarg you see to be sure it's not yours.
   c. Shout your flarg's name and see if he comes.
   d. Send out an All-Galaxy Bulletin: Missing Flarg!

Answers:
1. C is the best answer. In a, you're studying, which is responsible, but by test time your brain will be all kerfrazzeled. B is a terrible choice because you're not even studying! And d is bad, too. If you really need a nap, set the alarm on your ultra-krotal time keeper.
2. Both b and d are good answers (even if d is embarrassing) because they'll both get you to the right planet so you can do your job. A could take a l-o-n-g time. C is not responsible—and not honest, either.
3. I like d. You're accepting responsibility, and you're trying to make up for losing your friend's kicklride. In b, A is mean—and dishonest! In b, you're not being responsible, plus you're asking your friend to believe a crazy story. C is okay, but c and d together are best. You do owe your friend an apology, but that doesn't make up for leaving her with no kicklride.
4. Your best bet is d. All the Scouts in the galaxy will be looking for your flarg! C is good if you think your flarg is nearby. I don't like a, because you don't know that somebody stole your flarg—and you'll get the Galaxy Patrol all excited. B will get a lot of scouts annoyed at you!

• 59 •

FIND THE FLARG

I keep leaving things at my Earthling training center —and I can't find them when I go back and look! Can you help me out?

Stuff I forgot: Two globs of Gloop, Galaxy Scout training manual, Galaxy Scout Badge, pod, extra uniform, two extra boots, flarg

MEET THE AUTHOR AND ILLUSTRATOR

KIMBERLY MORRIS has written books about kids, dogs, fairies, and monsters, but writing about a third-grade alien with his very own spaceship is TOTALLY COSMIC. She lives in Texas with two dogs and a variety of unidentified flying insects.

JESSICA WARRICK has illustrated lots of picture books about dogs, cats, and kids, but she is mostly interested in drawing aliens, for some strange reason. She does a pretty good job acting like an Earthling . . . most of the time.

Spork just landed on Earth, and look, he already has lots of fans!

★ **Moonbeam Children's Book Awards Gold Medal**
Best Book Series—Chapter Books

★ **Moonbeam Children's Book Awards Silver Medal**
Juvenile Fiction—Early Reader/Chapter Books
for book #1 *Spork Out of Orbit*

"Young readers are going to love this series! Spork is a funny and unexpected main character. Kids will love his antics and sweet disposition. Teachers and parents will appreciate the subtle messages embedded in the stories. The kids in the stories genuinely like each other, which I found refreshing. I will be giving these books to my young friends."—**Ron Roy**, author of A to Z Mysteries, Calendar Mysteries, and Capital Mysteries

"A breezy, humorous lesson in honesty that never stoops to didacticism. The other three volumes publishing simultaneously address similarly weighty lessons—lying, shyness, bullying, and responsibility—all with a multicultural cast of Everykids. . . . A good choice for those new to chapters."
—**Kirkus** for book #1 *Spork Out of Orbit*

"This is a book where readers, kids, and aliens learn together, experiencing how words and choices affect all of us. It's simple, elegant, and very insightful storytelling. *Greetings, Sharkling!* doesn't waste a single page of opportunity."
—**The San Francisco Book Review**

"I'm so glad Spork landed on Earth! His misadventures are playful and sweet, and I love the clever wordplay!"
—**Becca Zerkin**, former children's book reviewer for the *New York Times Book Review* and *School Library Journal*

"Kids will love reading about Spork. Parents, teachers, and librarians will love reading aloud this series to those same kids."—**Rob Reid**, author of *Silly Books to Read Aloud*

How to Be an Earthling
Winner of the Moonbeam Gold Medal
for Best Chapter Book Series!

Respect

Honesty

Responsibility

Courage

Kindness

Perseverance

Citizenship

Self-Control

To learn more about Spork, go to kanepress.com

Check out these other series from Kane Press

Animal Antics A to Z®
(Grades PreK–2 • Ages 3–8)
Winner of two *Learning* Magazine Teachers' Choice Awards
"A great product for any class learning about letters!"
—*Teachers' Choice Award reviewer comment*

Let's Read Together®
(Grades PreK–3 • Ages 4–8)
"Storylines are silly and inventive, and recall Dr. Seuss's *Cat in the Hat*
for the building of rhythm and rhyming words."—*School Library Journal*

Holidays & Heroes
(Grades 1–4 • Ages 6–10)
"Commemorates the influential figures behind important American
celebrations. This volume emphasizes the importance of lofty ambitions
and fortitude in the face of adversity…"—*Booklist* (for *Let's Celebrate Martin
Luther King Jr. Day*)

Math Matters®
(Grades K–3 • Ages 5–8)
Winner of a *Learning* Magazine Teachers' Choice Award
"These cheerfully illustrated titles offer primary-grade
children practice in math as well as reading."—*Booklist*

The Milo & Jazz Mysteries®
(Grades 2–5 • Ages 7–11)
"Gets it just right."—*Booklist*, starred review (for *The Case
of the Stinky Socks*); *Book Links'* Best New Books for the Classroom

Mouse Math®
(Grades PreK & up • Ages 4 & up)
"The Mouse Math series is a great way to integrate math and literacy into
your early childhood curriculum. My students thoroughly enjoyed these
books."—*Teaching Children Mathematics*

Science Solves It!®
(Grades K–3 • Ages 5–8)
"The Science Solves It! series is a wonderful tool for
the elementary teacher who wants to integrate reading
and science."—*National Science Teachers Association*

Social Studies Connects®
(Grades K–3 • Ages 5–8)
"This series is very strongly recommended…."—*Children's Bookwatch*
"Well done!"—*School Library Journal*

KANEPRESS.com